DARK DREAMS

TALES OF TERROR

OTHER LIVING DEAD PRESS BOOKS

OTHER BOOKS IN THIS SERIES

THE DEADWATER SERIES

DARK DREAMS
TALES OF TERROR

EDITED BY
REBECCA BESSER

DARK DREAMS: TALES OF TERROR

Table of Contents

THE HAUNTED LIBRARY
CHARLES VERSFELT

"You killed me."

The weak, raspy whisper came to Addie like the chill from a slightly opened window, so faint that she almost didn't hear it. She turned, peering between the books. A boy of about five stood near the old fireplace in the children's section. His eyes were red and ancient looking, with large black circles around them. He held out his arms as if he wanted a hug. Just then Addie's brother came in, laughing and acting up as usual.

"Dave, this isn't a playground," Addie said. "Act your age. You're ten, not two. Besides, you'll frighten the boy."

"*What boy?*" Dave laughed. "There's no one else here."

Addie turned back, astonished. "But, I saw him!"

"This isn't about what that stupid gypsy said, is it? *You are sensitive to spirits. You have the power to see.* Yeah, you're seeing things all right!"

"You're not funny," Addie said, but that *was* pretty close to what the palm reader had told her the Saturday before on their trip to Seaside Heights' boardwalk.

"Perhaps you saw our resident spirit," Mrs. Rinehart said softly. Addie jumped, startled, and turned to see the librarian looming behind them.

She was a nice old lady, Addie thought, but she was quiet as a blade of grass and had a way of sneaking up on you when you weren't expecting it. Mrs. Rinehart adjusted her black, horn-rimmed spectacles, which looked like they were from another century.

"I've never seen any ghosts myself, of course," the librarian added. "The mind can play tricks on the imagination. But there *are* stories. . ."

"It *wasn't* my imagination," Addie insisted.

"Dave? Addie?" Mom called from the lobby. "I'm ready!"

Mrs. Rinehart raised her eyebrows, glancing toward the sound of Mom's voice. Then she leaned forward and whispered to Addie. "There's a Haunted Library tour on Friday, if you'd like to learn more about the legends."

2

Addie could barely contain her excitement. "I'll be here!"

*　*　*

That Friday, a group of children stood near the old fireplace, chatting merrily. Dave joined them. Addie stood in the back looking around uncomfortably. Soon, Mrs. Rinehart arrived. She distributed goodie bags filled with bookmarks, candies, and a tiny plastic flashlight to use later in the attic.

"*Is* the Raritan Library Haunted?" she began. "Some believe that it is. Our library's history goes back before the American Revolution. Somerset Street was then called Old York Road, and it was the main thoroughfare through New Jersey, connecting Philadelphia and New York. George Washington and his troops spent the winter of 1779 at the nearby Somerville's Wallace House. Dutch settlers built this house in the early 1700s, when Raritan was part of Bridgewater Township. It served as a tavern, a meeting hall, and even a jail! For years there have been stories of ghost sightings."

At that, Addie glanced in the corner. She almost fainted. The ghost boy stood right where he had been the last time! Addie lifted her hand, pointing toward the boy, but all eyes were on the librarian.

"In 1760, Frederick Frelinghuysen, a Colonel in the Revolutionary Army, bought the land," the librarian said. "He left it to his son, General John Frelinghuysen, who fought in the war of 1812. Addie, did you have a question?"

Addie looked back at the fireplace, but the boy was gone. "Sorry. It's nothing," she said.

"Probably saw a ghost," Dave said, rolling his eyes.

The librarian smiled. "I've never seen anything, but some people do believe a ghost haunts the library. No one can agree whose ghost. General Frelinghuysen died in 1833, leaving his house to his daughters, Sarah and Katherine. Katherine died in 1923, when she was ninety-four years old. The house went to a niece and nephew. They sold it to the Glacier family in 1924, who owned it until 1970, when Peter Frelinghuysen bought the house and donated it to Raritan Borough for use as a library and museum.

"Some people say they heard voices, or saw red, glowing eyes in our attic. Some say that a mysterious library keeper turns on lights, moves books, and opens doors at night, or that an old woman romps about in the garden. What *you* choose to believe is up to you. There are creaking boards and gaps in the wood floors that can cause sounds and movements of light that may seem ghostlike. Now, let's move our tour upstairs, to the Basilone room."

As the librarian led the children toward the staircase, Addie felt a chill on her back. Holding her hand near the fireplace, she noticed a cool breeze blowing between the bricks where the boy had stood. She flashed her light inside. There was something between the bricks, buried in dust! Using a bookmark, she coaxed it to the edge. Finally, she snatched out an old, black-and-white photograph.

A family stood at a door, a woman in a large frilly dress, a balding man with a bow tie and suspenders, and the ghost boy! Excited, Addie ran upstairs to show the group.

* * *

Mrs. Rinehart stood in the Basilone room, showing the children pictures of Raritan's World War II hero,

John Basilone. Addie burst into the room. Every head turned toward her.

"Addie! Where were you?" the librarian asked.

"I found this," she said, holding out the picture.

"Interesting," said the librarian. "This looks like our lobby, perhaps in the 1920s. I've seen similar pictures from the time. I don't recognize the family. They may have been friends of the Frelinghuysen or the Glacier families."

"I've seen that boy," Addie said.

"Maybe you saw someone who looked like the boy," Mrs. Rinehart suggested. "*This* boy would be a very old man by now, if he's still alive. We can talk about it after the tour. Now, let's move into our audio-video room."

The group followed her into what looked like a dining room with a long table in the center. Cases of recorded books and audio-video equipment lined the wall. Over the fireplace was the portrait of an eerie-eyed young woman.

"This is Katherine Frelinghuysen, probably before her father's death," the librarian said. "This room is thought to be haunted. Watch how the door swings by itself."

She held the door open, and then let go. The door swung slowly, hinges creaking. Just before it closed, Addie gasped. On the other side of the door, the boy stood, face pale, gray blood on his shirt. The children laughed.

"Ooh, a closing door, scary," Dave taunted her.

"Didn't you see?" Addie asked

"See what? It's just a door!"

"Addie, if this is too upsetting, you can wait in the lobby," Mrs. Rinehart said, opening the door.

"No, that's all right," Addie sighed, looking out into the hallway. The boy stood, gesturing for her to come.

"Wait. Maybe I will go," she said, slipping out and running after the boy. He turned back, beckoning.

She followed him, stomping her feet as her anger grew. No one ever listened to her. With Dave taunting her, no one would believe her even if she tried to explain.

The boy led her to the end of the hallway, into a room lined with bookshelves, and then through a small door into a storage area. The uneven floor tilted awkwardly, making Addie feel dizzy and disoriented.

"You killed me here," the boy said.

Addie noticed how pale the boy's skin looked, like in an old horror movie she had seen about zombies rising from the grave.

"I've never been here before," she said, trying to reason with the ghost. "I couldn't have killed you."

"You brought me to the attic," he said. He walked right through her, and then through the wall, back into the hallway.

Addie followed him up the narrow attic stairs, her plastic light casting a pencil thin beam before her.

She peered into the cold, filthy attic. Cobwebs were everywhere. Turning, Addie saw a figure and nearly screamed! It was a mannequin. Behind it, the boy pointed at the crumbling brick wall.

"You killed me. You put me here."

"Stop saying that," Addie said, terrified. "It's not true! I wasn't even born yet!"

She reached out and felt the wall. The bricks were powdery, brittle from years of decay. One brick was loose. It fell behind the wall, followed by another. Addie stepped back. There was a sound behind her, footsteps on the stairs. Then the whole wall collapsed violently.

From behind the wall, a skeleton fell just inches from Addie's face, a fat black spider crawling from its eye socket.

* * *

Addie awoke in Mrs. Rinehart's office, feeling dizzy. She rubbed her eyes and then felt the big knot on the back of her head. A few minutes later Mrs. Rinehart came in.

"I've called your parents," the librarian said. "They'll be here soon. You've been through quite an ordeal."

"What. . .what happened?" Addie asked. "The last thing I remember is a skeleton."

"The police are moving the remains now," Mrs. Rinehart said. "They found the diary of a widow named Henrietta Clarence dated 1923. Apparently, Katherine Frelinghuysen's niece briefly took in Mrs. Clarence and her son, Harry. Her husband had died in World War I. Afterward she courted a man, but he didn't want any children. Harry hated the man, said he wasn't his father, insisted on calling him by his first name. Then, one day the boy disappeared. The mother blamed the man and broke off their engagement. Months later he was found dead on the other side of town. He'd hanged himself. The skeleton appears to be that of the son."

"That's terrible!" Addie said.

"At least he'll get a proper burial now. We found the story in some old newspapers. Even then they suspected the man, Hugh Ames. Apparently he really did kill the boy."

"Hugh Ames?" Addie asked. "His name was *Hugh*?"

"That's what the police say," Mrs. Rinehart said.

"*Hugh* killed me," Addie said. "Now it makes sense."

There was a knock at the door. Dave came in, peering cautiously around at Addie.

"Addie! Are you all right?"

Addie shrugged. "Little bump on my head. No big deal. I suppose you'll tease me about it though."

"Tease you? Are you kidding? You rock!"

"What?" Addie asked.

"All the kids are talking about it! How you went into the attic all by yourself; how you found that skeleton. You're like a hero!"

She put her arm around him. "Thanks, little brother."

At that moment she heard a sound out in the hallway. She watched as a small boy passed by, red stains all over his hands and his shirt. The boy gave her a puzzled look.

"What are you looking at?" the boy asked, taking a red lollipop out of his mouth and sticking it back in his goodie bag, rubbing his hands on his shirt.

"Nothing," Addie said, realizing that he was a real boy. She heaved a sigh of relief. She thought Dave would laugh, but instead, he put his arm around her shoulders, and it occurred to Addie that the nightmare was finally over.

*   *   *

Author's Note: Although the characters in this story and the people and events surrounding the murder are fictional, the library and the rest of its history are real. Rumors of ghost sightings, glowing eyes in the attic, a ghostly library keeper and a spectral woman that walks the grounds, continue to this day.

MOON MIST
COURTNEY RENE

I hated going to Grandfather's farm. Hated, hated, hated it. We made the trip once a month, every month. The farm was out in the middle of nowhere. There was nothing to do and no one to play with.

That day, we had already been at the farm for hours and I was bored out of my mind. My mom had said, "Go outside and play, Sara." With what and who, was what I wanted to know.

I stomped my way out the back door and into the huge yard, surrounded by corn fields. I flopped down on my stomach in the over-long grass and closed my eyes.

It was a scorcher, low nineties, and very humid. Thankfully a breeze blew now and then, caressing and chilling my sweat dampened skin. The sun was on its way down, it wouldn't be long before it set for the day.

The bugs were going crazy all around me. I listened to the grasshoppers and crickets singing up a storm. Every now and again bees would go zipping past. There was cawing from the obnoxious crows out in the corn. They were too loud. Their noise bothered my ears, and I wished they would shut up.

That was just what they did too. I cracked open my eyes a bit when I noticed everything was suddenly silent. The setting sun had turned the world around me orange and purple.

I turned over, sat up, and looked around. Everything was haloed with the shadows of the falling night. It was creepy, especially the thick fog that was gently sweeping over the corn stalks and heading my way.

It would soon flow right over me, blurring the world from my sight, as well as me from the world. I stood up to see it better. It was barely tipping over the last row of corn when it stopped, like it had come to a wall and was unable to go any further.

I lifted my arm and reached out to touch it. Just as I was about to caress the white dew, I hesitated. I thought I heard something, a whisper of sound. I leaned forward and strained my ears. There it was again. It was someone calling out, "Come and play with us. Come and play."

I didn't see anyone. I squinted and focused on the fog, but I still didn't see anyone.

"Where are you?" I yelled into the darkening field.

I thought I saw something, someone. It was a dark shadow that clashed with the white mist.

"Sara, come play."

When I heard my name whispered on the wind, I drew back. I didn't know anyone here. Who would know my name?

"Mama?" I called out, thinking that maybe she had seen the fog and come looking for me.

I knew it wasn't her when the laughter drifted to my ears, raising goose bumps on my now chilled skin.

"No. Come and play, Sara. In the children's mist, come and play."

I again lifted my arm and reached forward. This time I pushed my hand through the barrier and into the fog. It felt cold and damp. I only had a moment to think about it, as almost immediately the mist flowed over me, all the way up to and past the house.

I watched it in utter shock as it ran in waves across the yard. It seemed to suck up everything as it went. It swallowed the house, erasing it from my sight. I knew it was still there, but not even a hint of light shown through the thick white dampness.

I turned back to where the cornfield should have been and listened. The laughter and the whispering were louder, getting closer, and I was suddenly afraid. I backed up several steps, tripped over the long grass, and fell down.

I scrambled to my feet, disoriented and not sure which way to run. The shadows in the mist were getting closer. They were not just coming from one point, but from all directions, surrounding me.

They continued to whisper to me, "Come play with us."

"Who are you?" I shouted. My words bounced back to me, off the shroud of white.

"The children of the mist," they echoed.

My heart was pounding in my chest. I was gasping, and couldn't breathe. There was too much water in the air. I was drowning.

My vision blurred and I fell to the ground, landing on my hands and knees, sucking in air as fast as I could. Like smoke in a fire, it wasn't as thick close to the ground. I gulped in as much air as I could.

"Sara," said the whispers.

I looked up, and saw the shadows take shape, one by one. Boys and girls of all different ages formed before my eyes. They were without color, grey like the mist. Their eyes were big black orbs. They were dead eyes. Their arms extended toward me, trying to grab me as they advanced toward me, still asking me to play.

I crab walked backwards on the ground, trying to get away from them. They just opened their black mouths wide and screeched with evil laughter. Still they advanced and tried to grab me.

I scrambled up, turned, and ran as fast as I could in what I thought was the direction of the house. When I ran into a wall of corn stalks, I realized I'd gone the wrong way.

"Sara!" The children shouted, getting closer and closer.

"Sara!"

I didn't hesitate, I turned and ran. I held my hands out in front of me to avoid running into anything, and succeeded except for when I stumbled over some plants on the ground.

Finally, I saw light showing through the thickness. I made a beeline directly for it. Racing up the steps to the back door, I wrenched open the screen and fell inside. Scooting quickly backwards, I kicked the door shut with a loud slam. Rising up to my knees, I hurriedly slid the bolt into place.

"What are you doing?" Mom asked, as she came out of the kitchen to investigate the noise.

I was still kneeling on the floor, panting, gasping for air, and shaking like a leaf.

Grandfather took one look at me and started laughing. Loud booming guffaws that embarrassed and enraged me.

"Did the fog give you a fright, girlie?" he asked and laughed again.

"There's something out there. In the mist," I said, indignant and offended.

"Nah," Grandfather said, looking out the window at the thick fog. "There's nothing out there. Don't worry about it. You know, it used to creep me out when I was kid too. Hmm. . . That's strange. It's never come up to the house before. It usually stops at the fields."

"I saw something," I said, trying to get them to listen.

"Oh, Sara," Mom said, rolling her eyes and shaking her head as she went back to the kitchen.

They wouldn't listen to me. I tried to tell them.

Grandfather said, "Calm down. It will be gone in a little while. It never stays long. You'll see. There's nothing out there."

True to his word, the mist faded away soon thereafter. It gave way to a clear full-mooned night, and Grandfather was right, there was nothing out there. . . then, but there had been. I know what I saw. Now, when we go to visit Grandfather at the farm, I'm always inside when darkness falls. The mist still comes, but it stops at the edge of the field. I don't listen for the whispers, and I don't watch for the children. I don't want to go out and play.

FAIRY DECEPTION
REBECCA BESSER

I was reading in the back yard, on the hammock, when I saw the first brilliant flash of color. At first I thought it was just the sun reflecting off of my Mom's metal wind chimes, but soon it was apparent by their movement and repeated appearance that it was something more.

Closing my book, I swung my feet over the side and sat up.

There were a dozen colorful lights weaving through the garden and flitting over the lush green grass of the back yard.

Standing, I ventured closer to get a better look.

They were fairies!

At first, I could do nothing but stare with my mouth hanging open. Then they spotted me and came closer, swirling around me.

Laughing, I held out my hands and a couple of them fleetingly landed on my palms and looked at me with interest, before taking off again.

I could hear them talking, but their little voices were too high pitched and faint for me to understand.

I stepped forward.

They stopped chattering and backed away.

"Oh, don't leave," I said. "I won't hurt you."

One of them fluttered forward and landed on my shoulder.

"Hello," he said in my ear. "Would you like to come see our home and play with us? It's not far."

"I don't know. My dad said that I shouldn't leave the yard."

"Why?" he asked.

"I don't know. He just told me that I couldn't go into the woods by myself."

"You would be with us," he said. "You wouldn't be alone."

I thought it over for a moment, that was true, I wouldn't be alone.

"We'll even show you the way back when you're ready," the fairy said.

I shrugged, almost knocking the fairy over. "Okay, I'll go with you."

The fairies all cheered. The one that was on my shoulder flew over to the others. Forming a circle by joining hands, they spun around me singing.

I laughed with joy, enjoying their presence.

They stopped spinning and flew off toward the woods, saying, "Come with us, play with us." Their voices blended together creating an eerie high pitched echo that gave me chills.

As I stepped from the green lawn onto the dark, soft floor of the forest, I had a moment of misgiving. Looking back at the house I wondered if I should tell someone where I was going.

I was just about to step back and go to the house, to leave a note, when a little pink fairy flew in front of my face and told me to hurry.

I smiled at her and followed them deeper into the woods. With each step I felt lighter, calmer. I forgot about home and what my dad had said.

The forest was dark at first, but as we went further, the trees thinned and sunlight shown through the green leaves of various shades. Ferns and flowers grew on the ground where the sun bathed the dirt with warmth.

I let go of my cares with a laugh and began dancing, spinning, and singing with the fairies.

Soon, we came to a clearing that had a teardrop-shaped pond in the center. It shimmered yellow as the rays of the sun danced across its rippling surface.

The fairies showed me their home by the pond and invited me to sit in the tall grass that grew around the water.

"Rest," they echoed. "We'll be back with a drink for you."

They fluttered away giggling amongst themselves, only to reappear moments later carrying a large cup between them. The cup was made of leaves woven together and held an orange liquid.

"What is it?" I asked as I took the cup.

"Juice," one fairy said.

"Made from fruit and flowers," said another.

"It's good, try it," insisted a third.

I brought the cup up to my nose and sniffed it. It smelled like an exotic fruit punch. I sipped it gingerly and was pleased to find it sweet and refreshing.

The fairies laughed and fluttered off to dance on the surface of the water, singing a song I couldn't understand.

I was thirsty after my walk and it didn't take me long to finish my drink. As I took the last sip, I began to feel drowsy. The harder I tried to keep my eyes open the more I felt like sleeping.

"I'm so tired," I muttered.

One of the fairies, a purple one, hovered in front of my face.

"It's the juice," she said. "You'll sleep until it's time, and then you'll awake, and be the sacrifice."

* * *

When I woke up, I was tied to a tree on the far side of the pond. My hands were bound behind me on the other side of the tree trunk. The rough, dark bark scraped against my bare arms as I struggled, burning them and breaking the skin.

I whimpered, tears springing to my eyes. I couldn't speak; there was some kind of vine gag in my mouth.

The fairies were on the ground by the pond. When they heard me moving around, they turned to look at me. Their sweet pixie faces were replaced with sinister smiles and hateful scowls.

I fought harder, whimpering louder.

They laughed harshly, some telling me to be quiet.

The fairy that had talked to me in my yard, the one that had convinced me to come with them, flew up to talk to me.

"You should stop fighting," he said. "There's nothing you can do. In the last few moments of the sunset, Agog will come and eat you. You're our sacrifice for this year and will keep our end of the peace treaty."

My mind was spinning. What was an Agog? What peace treaty?

"It's time," one of the other fairies called, and the deceiver went back to the others.

They all joined hands, creating a long line, and began weaving into strange shapes, swirling and twisting around each other, some of them fluttering into the air to accommodate the strange formations.

As they moved they chanted what sounded like a curse or a spell:

When the moon is but a sliver,
Agog comes to the bank with a quiver.
A sweet sacrifice to devour,
as the sun burns its last evening hour.
Agog will have his own way,
and peace between us will stay.
He cannot be escaped or beaten,
unless strong love protects the eaten!

As the last word of the curse was chanted, the fairies separated and flew straight at my face. Each one slapped or scratched my cheeks as they darted past, before hiding above me in the tree branches.

Just as the last fairy disappeared from sight the water in the center of the pond began to bubble, the bubbles grew bigger and reached further out, growing until they consumed the entire pond. The water began to steam as the whole pond came to a raging boil.

I fought harder and harder to get away. The bonds and tree cutting deeper, until I wasn't just crying from fear, but pain as well.

I kept my eyes trained on the water in front of me and froze in horror as a long maroon horn emerged from the boiling surface. It was followed by a head that faced the sunset.

A low rumble broke forth from Agog's large mouth as he stretched in the last rays of the sun. It was so loud the ground beneath my feet shook and I thought my ear drums would explode.

I took a step forward and yanked my arms with the weight of my body, succeeding only in tightening the ropes around my wrists and nearly dislocating my shoulders.

I cried out in pain, and that was when he turned his attention to me.

The horn that had first emerged stuck out of the left side of his head and curved toward the sky, ending in a sharp point. That side of his face was also maroon and looked like melted candle wax. It hung in loopy, shiny clumps down his whole left side. His maroon hand had three long, thick fingers, each ending in a four-inch curved claw. His left leg looked like an ostrich's, long, bony, thin, bending toward his back. His foot was similar to his hand, with claws to match.

The other side of his face, the right side, was an olive green color and was scaly like a lizard. The skin was tight against his muscles. His right arm was short, ending in a paw like a dog, a suction cup where each pad should've been. His right leg had fins hanging from it and the foot was the same as the hand.

Agog had only one eye. It was the size of a baseball and shimmered silvery-yellow. The orb wiggled in the middle of his two-toned face as he looked around. His mouth was where his neck met his chest. When he opened it, it looked like a slime-covered umbrella opening its folds to make a huge circle that was lined with multiple rows of sharp, ivory teeth.

He moved toward me, skimming his way through the water like he had all the time in the world.

The stench of puss and guts floated on the breeze in my direction, making me gag. I turned my head and closed my eyes, trying to forget the sight of him and get some fresh air. It was impossible. His stench filled the entire clearing.

When I chanced a look to check his progress, I was shocked to see that he was now lumbering up the bank.

I yanked harder and harder on my wrists, trying frantically to get them free.

Agog was close enough that I could feel his breath on my face.

I gagged, closing my eyes again.

I felt the skin of his face brush my cheek and I heard him sniffing me as he growled deep in his throat.

His paw hand gripped the side of my neck. The suction cups felt wet and sticky against my skin.

My eyes flew open at the contact to see his other arm reach behind me.

He sliced the rope with his claws, nicking my hand in the process. He sniffed the air and growled louder as he licked my blood from the tip of his long black talon.

I nearly fainted as his lime green tongue darted out inches from my face. It was split on the end and reminded me of a snake's.

Agog closed his eye as he savored the sample of my blood and the suction on my neck loosened.

I took the little chance that presented itself in his slackened grip. I jerked suddenly to the side, and with a loud smacking noise, I was loose from his paw.

I fell to the ground with the force of my extraction and quickly scrambled to my feet.

Agog roared and dove after me, narrowly missing my leg in his attempt to recapture me and make me his meal.

I ran into the tall grass that surrounded the pond, dropping down to my hands and knees so that he couldn't see me. Each time I pressed my injured palm down, dirt and small stones ground into it, making me wince. Despite the pain, I knew I couldn't slow down or Agog would catch up with me.

I heard him behind me and crawled faster. His roars alternated with snorts as he tried to catch my trail. I figured I didn't have a lot of time, my broken skin leaving my scent in blood for him to follow.

After crawling as fast as I could for a few minutes, I lifted my head above the grass to see how far I was from the woods.

The tree line was barely five feet to the left.

I chanced a look back to check Agog's progress, and was shocked to see him moving fast through the grass with his head down. If I darted into the woods now I would risk being seen, but I might get lucky enough that he would be looking at the ground and miss seeing me altogether.

Drawing in a deep breath I jumped up and ran for the cover of the forest. Just as I was passing the first tree my foot landed on a dry branch, the loud snap as it broke notifying Agog that I was now up and running.

With another angry roar he lunged across the rest of the clearing to pursue me.

No longer caring if I was heard, I doubled my speed. It didn't make a difference. He was bigger and faster. The ground shook with each of his heavy footfalls.

He was close behind me now, swiping at me with his claws. They caught in my shirt and sliced off chunks of my long hair as it bounced on the wind behind me.

I yelped and stumbled as one of his claws made contact with my neck, cutting it deeply.

Up ahead was a thick stand of briars. I pumped my legs as hard as I could, heading right for them. At the last moment, I dropped face down on the ground, scraping my cheek and bloodying my nose as I landed hard.

Agog looked down at me, not paying attention to where he was going, and fell into the briars, screaming as the little thorns bit into his flesh.

I jumped up and ran toward where I thought home would be, hoping that I'd picked the right direction.

Behind me I heard Agog thrashing and squealing like a pig as he tried to free himself from the bushes.

Soon, I felt the ground shaking as he made his escape and chased after me again.

I hid behind a large tree, breathing heavily. That's when I heard it. Someone was calling my name.

I looked around frantically, turning my head in every direction, trying to pinpoint where the voice was coming from.

I could hear Agog getting closer. I had to move or risk being discovered.

Jumping out from behind the tree, I ran in the direction that I thought the voice was coming from.

"Help!" I screamed.

Agog growled and changed direction to intercept me.

"Help!" I screamed again.

"Jessica!" a man's voice called.

"Dad," I cried out. "Help me!"

"Jessica," he yelled back. "Where are you?"

I heard him thrashing around and I changed my course to the right, toward the sound.

"Dad," I cried with relief as I saw him. "Agog is trying to eat me!"

"What?" he asked, confused. Then he looked behind me and saw the wild beast in pursuit. "What is that thing?"

I crashed into my dad's chest and he quickly ushered me behind him. He had his hunting knife with him and he drew it out of its sheath.

Agog came to a halt ten feet away, panting and growling, eyeing my dad. He opened his mouth wide, threw back his head, and roared.

Dad never took his eyes off the beast. "You can't have my daughter."

Agog roared again and stomped the ground in front of him. He stepped toward us, crossing half the distance.

"I said no!" Dad yelled and held the knife higher.

Agog bent forward and growled long, low, and deep, before lunging at us.

Dad pulled back and brought the knife up into Agog's chest as he wrapped an arm back around me, pushing me so that we stepped sideways together.

Agog missed us completely as he fell to the ground screeching.

I covered my ears and fell to my knees.

Pawing at his chest, Agog scurried off into the forest. It wasn't long before there was no sign of him. He was gone.

Dad turned around and looked down at me. He had tears in his eyes as he inspected my injuries.

"Oh, baby," he said and knelt down beside me, drawing me into his arms, hugging me gently. "Let's get you home."

Dad wrapped an arm around me and supported my weight as we stumbled home.

He never once scolded me for leaving the yard. He didn't have to. I'd learned my lesson. I know now that he only wanted to protect me.

Never again would I be deceived by the fairies.

The chant of those small demons danced though my mind that night as I was drifting off to sleep. The last line in particular, 'unless strong love protects the eaten!' My dad's love for me had given him the strength to save me from Agog. He'd saved me from being eaten.

HEARTLESS

CHARLES VERSFELT

Rachael stood shivering, her wide eyes pools of despair. "Ron, how do we kill a vampire that can't be killed?"

Wind whipped up the sand, battering the splintered wooden planks of the Seaside Heights boardwalk. The air was thick with the smell of sea spray. Cawing in harmony, seagulls danced over the crashing waves. The sun rose, a beautiful vision of red, yellow, and orange on a cloudy, blue-streaked horizon. The vampire had chased them here to the pier, but the sunrise forced it into a quick retreat. Tonight it would be on their scent again, like a wild wolf hunting its prey.

"How do we kill a vampire that can't be killed?" Rachael asked again. "How can we kill a vampire with no heart?"

"I don't believe it," Ron said. "It must be a trick. There has to be a way to kill it."

In his three months as Apprentice Vampire Hunter, Ron had seen five vampires destroyed by Rex's stake. Ron would never forget that day three months earlier when they had gone to visit his friend Jake Benton. Through the window they had seen a vampire draining Dr. Benton's blood with its murderous fangs. The vampire had turned and seen them, causing him and his sister Rachael to flee.

Rex had found them cowering on a nearby street.

"*Quickly,*" Rex had said. "*We must get away from here.*"

He led them for miles through a maze of back roads, before they had entered the woods where an ancient castle stood. It was the home of Rex Laird, the Vampire Hunter.

"*You'll be safe here,*" Rex had told them.

His castle was surrounded by a moat of wooden stakes, but Rex knew the children wouldn't be safe for long. The vampire had caught their scent and had targeted them. It would be far too dangerous for Ron and Rachael to return home. The vampire would track them down and kill them *and* their family. Until the vampire was destroyed, the children had to remain with Rex, hidden from the authorities and trained in the art of Vampire Hunting.

"*The only way to kill a vampire,*" Rex had told Ron during their first lesson, "*is to pierce its heart with a wooden stake. The sun will burn its skin and force it to flee, but it cannot kill a vampire. Its skin will heal as it sleeps.*"

"Ron!" Rachel cried. "What are we going to do?"

Ron shook off the memory. He turned, the sand burning his eyes. "I've lost my bearings. We ran so far that I don't know which way to go. Even if we figure out how to kill the vampire, I don't know how we'll find the cemetery where it's hiding!"

Rachael held up a small tracking device. "I have the location right here."

"That's Rex's GPS!"

"I grabbed it when we ran. It has the address of the vampire's cemetery programmed in."

"That was brilliant!" Ron said, smiling.

"Ron, you saw what happened! This vampire isn't like the other vampires! It. . . it has no heart! How can we possibly kill it?" Rachael started to cry.

"I know, I *know!* Let me *think!*" Memories pounded through Ron's brain, his own tears tracing salty paths down his face.

He could still see Rex as he lunged at the vampire, plunging the stake into its chest.

The vampire had gasped in mock terror and then burst out laughing, the stake jutting from its chest like a marcher's baton. Its voice was low, inhuman, as it growled, "*You can't kill a vampire that has no heart.*"

The bloodsucker had yanked the stake from its chest, tossed it aside, and then seized Rex, bearing its fangs.

"Rex didn't stand a chance," Rachael cried. "He died trying to protect us."

"It has got to be destroyed," Ron said.

"Hey, Kid!" a gruff voice said. "Try your luck?"

"Unbelievable," Ron said, turning to the left to see a sign saying: *Shell Game: Three tries for $2.00. Winner takes choice.* "First the night vampires disappear, then the day vampires come out looking for victims."

Ignoring the vendor, Rachael looked up at her brother "You're right. The vampire has to be destroyed. But, how?"

"Listen, Rach, I really need to think about this. Tell you what, why don't you play a few games? Here's two dollars. Maybe a quick break is what we need."

"Ron!"

"It's okay. We have time, and I still have the cash Rex gave me."

Rachael sighed as she took the money.

"Here, here," the vendor called, eyeing the cash. "Best odds on the boardwalk!"

"Of course you're the best odds. You're the only vendor open this early." Rachael said as she laid down the bills.

The vendor revealed a small black ball.

"You can't lose," he said, slipping the ball under one of three shells. "I'll show you right where the ball is. Follow the ball and you'll win the prize of your choice." He nodded at the large stuffed animals arranged behind him. His hands moved swiftly, swapping shells back and forth.

Watching the shells, Ron's mind returned to Rex's lessons.

"*Vampires prey on the weakest people,*" the Vampire Hunter had told Ron. "*The homeless, the poor, and orphans; people who are alone, who no one cares about.*"

"*That's heartless,*" Ron had said.

"That one!" Rachael said.

The vendor lifted the shell to the right.

"Sorry," he said, shaking his head and showing her the ball under the middle shell. "That's okay. You still have two more tries."

The vendor again shuffled the shells and Ron returned to his memories.

"*The vampires have no compassion,*" Rex had said, sharpening his stakes. "*They're filled with hate. Without hate a human will die at the taste of vampire blood, but the hateful are made strong. They rise again, becoming vampires themselves.*"

"There," Rachael said.

The vendor lifted the middle shell, which was empty, and then showed her the ball under the shell on the right. The last round began.

"I don't understand," Ron remembered telling Rex. *"If the vampires go after the poor and homeless, why did it kill Jake's father, a successful doctor?"*

"I don't know," the Hunter had admitted. *"Revenge, perhaps?"*

Rachael hesitated, eyeing the shell on the left. She started to gesture when Ron grabbed her hand. He pointed to the shell on the right.

"That shell," Ron said. "I saw you fake the last swap."

The vendor grinned, revealing the ball under the shell on the right. "Good eye, boy. We have a winner. Winner takes choice!" He took out a rubber snake, a tiny stuffed dolphin, and an even smaller stuffed bird, each no bigger than his pinky finger.

"Hey!" Rachael said. "Don't I get to pick from those big ones?"

"Those?" The vendor looked surprised. "You get those after ten wins. You should have read the sign!"

The sign he mentioned was half hidden behind the prizes and was so small that they had to squint to read it.

"Just pick one Rachael, and let's go. I have an idea what we should do next."

Rachael grabbed the dolphin as Ron took her arm, pulling her away.

"Where are we going?"

"To visit Jake," Ron said. "Vampires rarely murder someone as well known as Dr. Benton. Jake might have some information that will help us."

* * *

Later, Ron pressed the doorbell of Jake's mansion. The home doubled as a doctor's office when Dr. Benton had been alive.

Leaning on crutches, Jake answered the door. He stood in slack-jawed amazement at the sight of his friends.

"Ron! Rachael! I haven't seen you in months! Everyone has been worried sick about you! Where have you been?"

"It's a long story, Jake. What happened to you?" Ron asked, pointing at the crutches.

"Sprained ankle. A soccer accident."

"I'm sorry to hear that. Can we come in?"

"Of course," Jake said. "Can I get you anything?"

"I'm starving!" Rachael said.

"Actually, neither of us has eaten," Ron said. "But we need to talk."

"My mom is out, but I can make you some sandwiches," Jake said. Over peanut butter and jelly sandwiches, they told him their story.

* * *

"You saw it?" Jake asked. "You saw the vampire that killed my dad?"

"We even have its location," Rachael said, holding up the GPS device. "Do you really believe us?"

"I knew it!" Jake said. "I knew vampires were real! The police just wouldn't listen! And one of the vampires. . ." He paused, his voice cracking with emotion. "It killed my Dad. . ."

"We think that *this* vampire had a reason to go after your father," Ron said. "Did your dad know anyone who was especially hateful?"

"Hateful?"

"You know. Someone mean tempered. Evil."

Jake thought about it for a moment. "Well, there was someone, one of his patients. . . Wait, come with me, to Dad's office! I'll show you his file!"

Jake led them to a side door, taking out his key. "His name was Kendrick Klong," Jake said, opening the door and leading them through clean rooms that smelled of alcohol. He pulled open the drawer of a metal filing cabinet and paged through the files. "He was in a car accident. Dad had to do emergency surgery. Klong accused Dad of messing up his operation. He threatened to sue! Dad said the operation wasn't his fault, that the man was abnormal from birth. Then, a short while later, he just disappeared."

"Probably when he became a vampire," Rachael said.

"We don't know that yet," Ron warned.

Jake dug frantically through the files. "It's not here!"

"What?" Rachael asked.

"The office was broken into after Dad was killed. Klong probably took it!"

"Could there be other copies somewhere?" Ron asked.

Jake shook his head. Then he stopped. "Wait. There's one possibility." He hobbled to a stack of mail on the end table. "There was something in the mail from Dad's lawyer. Mom set it aside. Here it is!" Jake handed the envelope to Ron.

Ron opened it and dumped out the contents. Out fell a photograph of Kendrick Klong.

"That's him!" Rachael cried. "That's the vampire!"

From the envelope, some typed court documents dropped onto the table. Behind them was a hard, transparent sheet that Jake recognized as x-rays.

"Here we go!" Jake said, lumbering to a board that looked like one Ron had seen on the television show *ER*. He slipped the x-ray into the board and turned on the light.

"It's the inside of his chest!" Jake said.

"He *seems* to have a heart," Ron said. "Perfectly normal, like everyone else."

"Then why didn't Rex's stake kill him?" Rachael asked.

"I don't know," Ron said. "Maybe something happened to his heart after the x-ray was taken, when he became a vampire. Maybe the vampire that turned Klong into a vampire somehow removed his heart. Let's read the papers. They might have a clue."

For nearly an hour they puzzled over the documents. When Ron finished, he crossed the room to the sink and washed his face. He looked into the mirror, his sad, tired face stared blankly back at him. The papers didn't make any sense. He was so tired he couldn't remember a thing he'd read. In the mirror he could see the x-ray across the room, Klong's name written on the side. His mind was spinning like the shells from that morning. Then it dawned on him.

"That's it!" he said.

Rachael ran to Ron. "Jake's gone!"

"What do you mean Jake's gone?"

"He took the GPS! I think he has gone after the vampire by himself!"

"He is going to get himself killed. We have to stop him!"

"I memorized the location," Rachael said. "I know where he went."

*　*　*

The light was fading on the horizon as the taxi dropped Ron and Rachael off at the cemetery.

"This is the place," Rachael said.

"I remember it," Ron said, looking desperate. "We don't have much time. The sun is almost down. We *have* to find Jake."

50

They ran deep into the cemetery toward the large stone building where the vampire lay hidden in an ancient stone coffin. In the distance they saw Jake on his crutches, moving between the buildings with surprising speed.

"Jake, wait!" Ron called, but he was too late.

Jake had already stepped into the building.

* * *

Jake opened the coffin. Inside, the vampire that was Kendrick Klong laid with eyes closed.

"This is for Dad," Jake said, raising the stake he had taken from Ron's bag.

The vampire opened his eyes and hissed.

Jake hesitated and the vampire grabbed his wrist.

Running at a blinding speed, Rachael smashed into Jake. The vampire lost his grip, Jake and Rachael tumbled down, the crutches clattering loudly against the stone floor. Ron ran up behind them with a sharpened stake raised.

"What do you think you're going to do with that?" Klong laughed. "You know you can't kill me!"

With all his might, Ron thrust the stake into the right side of the vampire's chest.

"He missed!" Rachael cried.

Klong's eyes widened and he bore his teeth with a hiss. "No!" he screamed. For a moment, he looked like a skeleton, as if they suddenly had x-ray eyes. Then he crumbled into dust, leaving behind nothing more than a wisp of smoke.

"It's over," Ron said. "The vampire is destroyed."

"How?" Rachael asked, looking confused.

"I was thinking about the shell game," Ron explained. "When I looked in the mirror at the x-ray, I realized I could read Klong's name in the reflection. That would have been impossible unless. . ."

Jake nodded, understanding. "Unless we were looking at the x-ray backwards!"

"The legal papers didn't make any sense to me. It was all legal mumbo-jumbo," Ron said. "When I saw the x-ray I remembered that Dr. Benton said that Klong was born abnormal. He must have been born with all his organs reversed! His heart was on the right side of his chest, not the left side like most people."

"I get it," Rachael said. "It's not that the vampire didn't *have* a heart. It's just that his heart wasn't in the right place."

"Like the shell game," Ron said. "Rex couldn't kill Klong because he stabbed him in the wrong place."

Jake hugged Rachael. "You saved my life, both of you. Thanks."

Ron smiled at his friend. "We're glad to help."

"At least *your* heart is in the right place," Jake said. "I guess you can go home now."

"Yeah," Ron said. "I miss Mom and Dad. Still, I don't think this is over for me."

Rachael looked at her brother. "What do you mean?"

"With Rex gone I'm the only one left to hunt Vampires. Now that I've destroyed a vampire I'm not an Apprentice anymore."

Ron took his sister's hand. Giving the fallen crutches to Jake, he gestured toward the stone door and the three walked outside. The last rays of sunlight faded in the distance, but the children were unafraid, for among them was a Vampire Hunter, capable of facing any danger they might encounter on their way home.

MIDNIGHT CLEARING
REBECCA BESSER

Alan slid the window open, flinching as it creaked.

He paused to see if the noise had woken his parents. When he didn't hear anyone moving around, he eased it the rest of the way up.

He dropped his pack out onto the ground, four feet below, and followed it out. Landing on the pack, Alan groaned as the flashlight inside dug into his ribs. Sitting up he rubbed his side and let his eyes adjust to the complete darkness of the outside world. Once he could make out the outlines of trees and could locate objects in the yard, he stood and began his journey.

Alan yawned as he wound his way down the quarter mile driveway, on his way to the black topped township road. He wondered what he'd been thinking when he'd agreed to this.

An owl hooted, its deep voice echoed loudly in the otherwise silent night.

He flinched, and sighed. Another half of a mile and he would be at the old bridge where Turner and Lyle were supposed to meet him.

Alan heard hushed voices before he saw the bridge. Walking around the last bend in the road he saw the two boys lounging on the ancient wooden planks.

"Oh, look," Turner said in a loud whisper. "The scared little baby made it."

Lyle laughed.

Alan clenched his jaw and kept walking until he was standing toe to toe with Turner. "I'm not a scared little baby."

Turner laughed. "Are you gonna prove it?"

"I'm here, aren't I?"

"Yeah, yeah, you made it," Lyle said. "But, that doesn't mean you aren't a scared little baby."

Alan turned to glare at Lyle. "I don't see any aliens around here. Unless you're one, which wouldn't surprise me."

"What's that supposed to mean, shrimp?" Lyle said, clenching his fists and taking a step in Alan's direction.

Alan stood his ground and stared at Lyle. He wasn't going to let him see that he was scared.

Turner laughed and placed a hand on Lyle's shoulder. "Don't let the little baby get you all wound up. He just wants you to beat on him so he won't have to be an alien's snack."

Lyle growled and turned away. "Maybe I'll beat him if they don't think he's good enough to eat."

A strong breeze blew up from the creek bed below, howling as it blew through the rotting boards, causing Alan to shudder. He was scared, but he wasn't going to admit it.

"So, where are these 'aliens' you two love to talk about?" Alan said with false bravado. "They at your houses? Keeping your moms company?"

"You better watch your mouth, shrimp," Lyle said. "Turner ain't big enough to stop me if I really want to get at you."

Alan looked down and smirked, knowing the darkness would hide his expression.

"After that comment," Turner said. "I won't stop Lyle from teaching you a lesson if the aliens don't take you."

Alan shrugged. "Whatever. We all know there are no aliens and that you two are just being jerks. Are we going to do this? Or should I go home and back to bed? I'm awfully tired." He yawned for show, shrugged, and started to walk away.

Turner grabbed his pack, spinning him around. "You aren't getting away that easy. We'll show you the spot. Let's go."

Turner turned on his flashlight, crossed to the far side of the bridge, and stepped into the woods.

Alan followed him slowly, pausing at the tree line, swallowing hard.

Lyle shoved Alan forward, almost making him fall to the ground. "Get moving, shrimp. We wouldn't want to be late for the light show, now would we?"

Alan hurried to catch up with Turner. He didn't want to be left alone in the dark with Lyle.

They twisted and turned through the night, around trees, over rocks, and through bushes. Finally they came to a small triangle-shaped clearing.

"This is it," Turner said, lifting his arms and spinning in a circle like he was showing off his own, personal grand achievement. "This is where the aliens like to come for a visit."

"Doesn't look like much," Alan said, shrugging.

"Oh, don't worry, shrimp, it'll look more interesting when your guests arrive," Lyle sneered.

"Remember, you have to stay here until one o'clock," Turner said. "They usually arrive around midnight. Lyle and I will be waiting at those rocks we passed, so we'll know if you chicken out."

"Yeah, I know," Alan said yawning. "I'll enjoy my nap in the woods."

"I bet you will, shrimp," Lyle said.

Turner and Lyle turned to go, grinning at each other.

"Oh," Alan called after them. "Lyle, did you want me to give your family a message, you know, when they arrive?"

Lyle turned toward Alan and walked backwards slamming his fist into the palm of his other hand.

Alan smiled and waved, pretending he didn't care that he was being left alone in the woods where beings from another world were supposed to come and visit.

Alan sat up against a tree and wrapped himself in the blanket he'd brought with him. He held his flashlight close to his chest, in case anything did show up. He thought the whole 'space beings' thing was silly. But, as he sat there in the dark, alone, his mind started making him wonder if there wasn't some truth to it.

Time passed slowly as the moon inched its way through the star-filled sky. Soon Alan became drowsy and fell asleep.

*   *   *

Bright lights were flashing. Loud beeps were sounding.

"Stop doing that with the lights, Mom, I'm getting up," Alan mumbled as he reached over to turn off his alarm. But, instead of a night stand his hand met air, and then dirt as he fell over. "What the. . .?"

Alan was instantly awake. His eyes opened wide as he looked around in confusion. The forest was ablaze with bright, white light that pulsed and moved like a living being. The beeping kept getting louder and louder, and he had to cover his ears as it hit a painful pitch.

Alan screamed, but his voice couldn't be heard over the deafening noise.

Looking up at the sky, Alan was shocked to see that there was an oval object floating above the trees. Steam rolled out from the center of it, creating an opening, but he couldn't see what or who was inside. His eyes couldn't filter out the light. It was too bright.

He tried to stand and keep his hands over his ears at the same time. But, he found this impossible and kept falling back to the ground. As he faltered the fourth time, the beeping stopped. The light also went out, plunging the world into blackness.

Alan stood and ran into the woods, tripping over a fallen tree. He decided to stay on the ground and hide. Pressing his body as close as he could against the trunk, he blinked rapidly, trying to get the light spots to disappear from his vision.

Moments passed, but it seemed like centuries to him. Alan heard something or someone moving around. The sounds of hissing and screeching kept getting closer and closer to his hiding place.

"It's one o'clock," Turner yelled, coming through the woods. "You can come out now."

The hissing stopped.

Alan gulped.

"Come on, shrimp," Lyle said. "Let's get your beating over with so you can go home."

Something shuffled on the other side of the log. Alan heard whatever was over there change direction and head toward Turner and Lyle. They were making a lot of noise coming through the woods; laughing together about the joke they'd played on him by making him stay in the forest alone and wait for aliens.

The shuffling got further and further away from Alan. He didn't know what to do. He still couldn't see. If he hollered to Turner and Lyle, to warn them, he would give away his position.

"Come on, Alan," Turner yelled. "I want to go home! It's late."

Turner and Lyle were getting closer.

Alan didn't hear anything close by and his sight was beginning to clear. Slowly, he flipped over onto his stomach and raised himself up to his hands and knees to peek over the log.

Alan saw too tall, dark shapes moving toward Turner and Lyle, who were clearly marked by the beams of their flashlights. The figures moved slowly, like they were trying to sneak. They stopped every now and again to look at their surroundings and sniff the air.

Turner and Lyle continued to laugh and joke loudly as they stomped through the woods.

Alan's heart was beating fast. He had to do something soon or the creatures would get Turner and Lyle. He had a fleeting thought of not bothering to save them. A world with two less bullies wouldn't be so bad. But, he just couldn't be that cruel.

When Alan thought the beings were far enough away from both his position and Turner and Lyle's, he jumped to his feet.

"Run! Aliens! Run!" Alan screamed and took off running back the way they'd come earlier.

The aliens screeched loudly.

Turner and Lyle screamed.

Alan heard someone running behind him and glanced over his shoulder, expecting to see Turner or Lyle. Instead he saw the moon reflect off of glossy black eyes and a wide open mouth with thin sharp teeth. The thing hissed when Alan stumbled and almost fell, but he retained his footing and kept going.

He focused on what was in front of him so that he didn't falter again. Faintly he could still hear Turner and Lyle screaming. They seemed to be moving in the same direction as he was, so Alan didn't worry about them. He'd done what he could. Now it was time to save himself.

The creature was gaining on him. He could hear its hissing getting louder.

Up ahead Alan could see the bridge where they'd met earlier and he pushed himself to speed up.

The alien hissed and clamped its teeth down on the hood of the sweat shirt he was wearing, shaking it violently. Alan fell to his knees and struggled free of the clothing. He jumped up and ran toward the bridge again, which was now only ten yards away.

The being let out a loud, angry sounding screech when it realized its prey had gotten away. It bounded after the small boy, intent of making him a meal.

Alan gasped as something scratched his ankle. He fell, tumbling into the creek bed, landing in the water with a splash. He turned over and looked up at the bank. The full moon was high in the sky, giving him his first good look at the alien.

It was tall and unbelievably thin. Its skin was a deep purple color, almost black. Its eyes were huge black orbs that moved around on its face as it looked in different directions. The thing's arms were very short, no more than a foot long, ending in a single long talon with a spiral curve on the end.

Throwing back its head, the creature screeched loudly, pacing on the top of the bank.

Alan was confused. Why didn't it come after him?

Lifting his hand, Alan wiped some water from his face. Not realizing the force of his movement, he accidentally threw a spray of water into the air.

The alien jumped back, screeching again.

Alan thought about it for a second and then stood up, letting the water flow around his ankles. "You don't like water do you?"

Taking a hand full of water, Alan flung it at the aggravated creature.

It jumped back with a low hiss.

Alan laughed and threw more water, making the alien back away another step.

"Turner! Lyle! Get in the creek! They're scared of water!"

Alan prayed that they were close enough to hear him as he continued to throw water at the menace on the bank.

A couple minutes later he heard two loud splashes on the other side of the bridge.

"Turner? Lyle? You guys okay?" Alan shouted, and was relieved to hear them say yes in reply. "Throw water at them! They don't like it!"

They stayed that way for hours, standing in the creek, throwing water at the aliens above.

None of them noticed the clouds gathering in the sky. They were too busy battling for their lives. The boys didn't even notice when it started raining. They were soaked and throwing water. The additional drops didn't register. But, the aliens noticed.

Each drop made their skin sizzle like it was burning. They screeched and spun around, clawing at their bodies as the rain assaulted them. Turning, they fled into the woods, back to their ship for safety.

When the boys thought they were gone, they crawled out of the creek on the opposite side. They lay gasping in the grass, exhausted.

Alan lifted his head to look at the woods and make sure the creatures were indeed gone.

One of them was standing just inside the tree line, watching the boys, ignoring the sizzle of its burning flesh. It watched Alan for a long moment, opened its mouth, and let out a loud, ear splintering screech that had all three boys covering their ears. Lifting its little arm it pointed its talon at Alan. It wiggled it a little as if it were waving, before it turned and followed the others.

Alan shuddered, wondering if he'd been singled out. Wondering if they would return for him someday.

* * *

A month later, Alan was out in his yard when he heard a faint hissing in the woods beyond the house. He looked up to see one of the aliens standing in the shadows watching him.

Slowly, Alan reached behind him and took out the water gun he'd tucked into the waist band of his pants. He waved it at the creature and squirted some water into the air. The stream of liquid sparkled in the bright sunlight, giving no doubt as to what it was.

Alan smiled as the alien backed up a step, shaking its head from side to side.

He never saw any of them again after that. But, he never went anywhere without a bottle of water or a squirt gun for a long time, just in case.

Turner and Lyle no longer picked on Alan. In fact they became his best friends, especially after no one believed the tale of their encounter. The three of them knew what was out there. They knew they had to stick together to be safe. No one else would come to their aid. . . if the aliens should return.

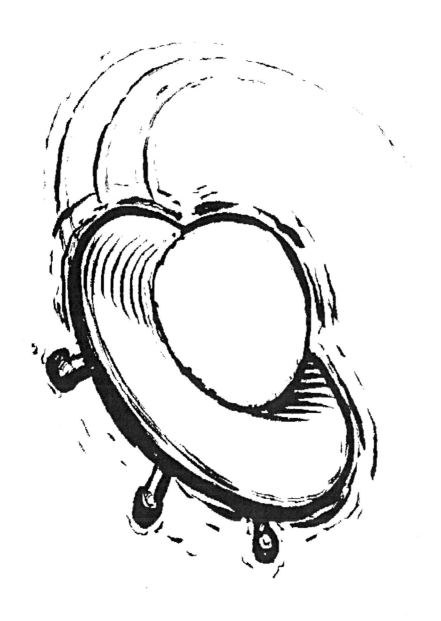

THE SHADOW OF DEATH
MIKKI SADIL

No one should ever take a dare.

We were hanging out on the front porch and complaining about what a bummer this summer was going to be. Forest was going to Jamaica with his parents to meet some relatives he'd never heard of; Talyn was being shipped off to some kind of summer camp to learn to play golf, which he hated but his father insisted he learn to play; Brianna was going on what she called a 'cruise with the snob mob', which meant she was going on a cruise with her very wealthy parents and some of their equally wealthy friends who had kids she couldn't stand. Me? I was going to sit home alone all summer. Well, not exactly alone. I had my little brother and sister, the *twin demons*, to babysit.

My know-it-all sixteen-year-old brother sauntered out of the house with a smirk and said, "I've got something for you bums to do. Go out to the woods at the edge of town and see if you can find that old mansion."

"What? Are you crazy, Reagan? Nobody walks through those woods at night. Nobody *ever* goes to that mansion." I poked him angrily.

"Oh yeah? Well, I dare you! No, I *double dare* you to go. You guys are always bragging about how you can do anything, well, do that! Unless you're just a bunch of cowards."

Forest and Talyn got up. "Hey, we're not cowards. Come on, let's go."

Brianna and I got up and looked at each other uneasily.

"Uh, Reagan, I don't think Mom and Dad would want us to do this," I said.

He smirked again. "Yeah, I figured you'd use them for an excuse. You're all a bunch of chickens." He flapped his arms and clucked as he went back inside.

Talyn said, "He *did* dare us, and I never back down from a dare. Come on, we can just walk to the edge of the woods. Reagan will never know."

That seemed like a sensible idea, and at least it was something to do. We left the porch and started walking. We got to talking and laughing, and didn't realize how far we'd gone. Our town is small, and it wasn't long before we were on a dark dirt road outside of the township limits.

We were at the edge of the woods. The moon went under a cloud and a cold wind began to wail among cruelly twisted tree branches that swayed in front of us, as if dancing to music we couldn't hear. The wind stopped and the night became as silent as death. There weren't even the usual night songs of crickets and tree frogs.

"We're here. Let's go back now," Brianna said.

"Wait a minute," Forest said. "Come on, let's just walk in a little ways. We don't have to go far."

"Heck, as long as we're here, we might as well go find that old mansion everyone says is haunted," Talyn said with a shaky laugh.

Brianna stopped in the middle of the road. She looked frightened. "No way, I'm not going. My mom says no one's ever stepped into that house since that lady and all those kids were murdered, and that nobody ever should."

"Come on, Brianna. Don't be such a scaredy-cat. I'm going, and so is Forest. What about it, Alexis, you coming with us?" Talyn was grinning at me.

Forest scowled and said, "Naw, I bet Alexis ain't coming. She's as big a coward as Bree is."

Nobody calls me a coward. I'm just as brave as any stupid ole' boy. "I am so coming. Bree, you wanna wait here?"

Brianna looked around and shook her head. "You guys are crazy, but I'm not staying out here alone. I'll come, but I don't like it."

We pushed through the brush, trying to find a path. There wasn't one. The trees were massive, tall and thick, with thin vines crawling up their trunks like lazy snakes looking for a place to sleep.

We hadn't gone far when Brianna said, "I don't like this. I think we should go back."

I agreed, but when I turned around I saw that the woods had closed behind us like an army surrounding its enemy. We couldn't see where we'd come from. We looked at each other, seeing our own fear mirrored on each other's faces.

Forest said, with a dash of bravado, "Come on, there has to be a path to the mansion. Let's find it, and we can get home from there."

Brianna and I shook our heads. We didn't understand his logic. Just because there *might* be a path to the mansion didn't mean there *would* be one leading back to town. But there didn't seem to be any other way out of the woods, so we followed the boys.

Before long, Forest yelled, "Look! I was right! There's the mansion, and here's a sidewalk. Come on, hurry up!"

The forest seemed to have magically parted, and a wide, crumbling brick sidewalk led from a mass of heavily entwined vines and bushes up to a huge, grotesque house. It leaned heavily to one side, as though someone - or something - unseen was holding it up. We could smell a stench even from this far away. Whatever it was it smelled of evil and death.

We crept up the sidewalk like we were spies on a mission. The iron gate protested loudly when we pushed it open, while the old house stared malevolently at us through the empty eyes of its windows.

Forest ran up the porch steps and opened the front door. A sliver of grey mist drifted out and a shiver began at the back of my neck and curled itself down my backbone.

Brianna hung back and whispered, "I don't want to go in there. I want to go home."

Talyn laughed. "See! I told you she wouldn't come. Don't be such a baby. It's just an old house that creaks and groans. Alexis, you coming? Or you gonna be a baby, too?"

I grabbed Brianna's hand and pulled her along. We stepped into the front room and the mist became a thick fog which surrounded us. It was heavy - thick like molasses - but at the same time cold and damp. I suddenly knew there was evil hidden in this house. My scalp prickled and goose bumps popped up on my arms. We couldn't see each other, but I was still holding Brianna's hand. Until something grabbed my other hand and pulled me away from her.

"Hey, Forest or Talyn, stop pulling me, you guys. What are you doing?"

They didn't answer me. I couldn't get my breath. I was being pulled by someone - or something - up a staircase. I tried to call out, but the words seemed to be hidden in some dark crevice of my brain. I was pushed into a room at the top of the stairs. The fog lifted. The door slammed shut. I reached out to open it, but there was no door knob. Fear, cold and slimy, slithered through my body like a thousand worms wiggling under my skin.

I pounded on the door but there was no sound. It was like my fists were hitting nothing but air. I thought my heart was going to explode with fear.

Okay, Alexis, calm down. Look around and figure out a way to get out of here. It's just an old house, nothing more.

I took some deep breaths and looked around the room. There were no windows, just an old Victorian bed with a beautiful white dress lying across it. A dark shadow splashed across the front of it. It smelled kind of sweet and yet, metallic. I walked over and touched it. It was wet, warm, and thick on my fingers. It was blood! I freaked and ran for the door. It opened by itself, but the stairs were gone. Only the hallway - and space - remained.

I stood in the hallway and yelled, "Hey, Forest? Talyn? Brianna? Where are you? I can't find my way down. Come get me, please!"

Only silence, darkness, and cold answered my plea. I was shivering, afraid to move. Then I heard it.

Whispers. Weeping. Voices.

"Alex. . .iiiiis! Alex. . .iiiis! Help us! Commeee heeereee, Aleee. . .xis, help us!"

Those tiny voices terrified me, but something was drawing me toward the sounds. I walked hesitantly forward and found myself in another bedroom, with seven tiny flickering candles dancing around as if carried by invisible pixies.

There were four cribs and three small beds in the room. All were white and were covered with the same dark stains as the dress had been. Blood was everywhere; splattering the floor as it dripped from the crib rails; pooling on the beds; creeping down the walls and inching its way toward my feet. It was as though the murders had just happened, rather than five years ago.

I started to cry as I realized I was in the room where the children were murdered. Their voices were still there; whispering; whimpering; pleading.

Then it was all over. The voices stopped. The house was deathly still.

I backed away from the horror in front of me. I turned to run, and she was there. The figure of a woman, only it was nothing but a pale blue outline without substance. A hand beckoned me, and without thinking, I started toward her. She pointed toward the bedroom, but abruptly, the house gave a horrendous moan and the figure evaporated. Before I could move the same cold fog from downstairs curled around me, tightening around my throat until I could barely breathe. I tried to scream again, but I couldn't force any sound out. I huddled against the wall, wondering how I would ever get out of this house. Wondering why I had ever agreed to come *into* this house. If I ever got home, I would never take another dare as long as I lived.

As suddenly as it had appeared, the fog was gone, and I yelled, "Forest, Talyn, Brianna! Answer me, darn it! This isn't funny! Where are you guys? Help! Help!"

There was nothing, not even an echo. Just. . .silence.

The figure appeared again, holding her hand out to me. What did she want? What could I do about the ghastly secrets hidden in this house? I was only thirteen, for Pete's sake, and I was scared to death.

I want to go home! I want my mother!

She approached me and I shrank away, but there was nowhere for me to go. She reached out and touched my face. I could feel the touch, but there was nothing to see except the mist that outlined her body.

She was gone. The mist was gone. The silence was gone. I heard laughing and chattering. The next thing I knew, Brianna, Forest, and Talyn had run up the stairs that had suddenly appeared from out of nowhere. They stopped and stared at me, horrified expressions on their faces.

"Alexis! What happened? We've been looking everywhere for you!"

Brianna's eyes were huge. "Oh my gosh, what's that stuff all over you?"

"Whaddya mean, stuff? That's. . . that's blood! Holy crap, Alexis, what happened?" Forest's voice was shrill and instead of coming toward me, he and Talyn were backing away.

"Please, let's just get out of here. I'll tell you when we get home. I want to leave, now!"

We turned around, but once more, the staircase had disappeared. There was nothing but space yawning up at us. Talyn looked at me, his eyes wide in a face suddenly gone white. Before he could speak, they came again. The voices; pitiful; whimpering; whispering; crying.

"Alex. . . iiis, help us. . . heeelllp us. . ."

The blue mist woman reappeared. None of us moved or said a word. The figure reached out and icy cold enveloped my hand as she drew me slowly down the hallway. I looked back and saw Bree and the boys tiptoeing behind me.

The bedroom door swung open and the bloody scene was there in front of us.

Brianna gulped and the boys gasped. This time the pools of blood by the cribs and beds were bigger, and in each of them lay a tiny white outline of a baby or small child.

I looked back at Brianna and the boys. Their eyes were wide in faces white with fear.

I heard Brianna whisper, "Alexis, come on, let's get out of here."

But I couldn't leave. Something was keeping me in the room. I looked back at the outlines and saw miniature tracks running through the blood. I stared at them, and before I knew what I was doing, I reached down and touched one of them. I put my finger to my lips. It was salty! Tears! The murdered children were crying.

I took a step forward and heard Talyn say in a shaky voice, "Al. . . Alexis, you're not. . . not going into that room, are you?"

I could see the shock on Brianna and the boys' faces. But the longer I looked at those tiny shapes on the floor; the more I heard their cries and whispers; the more my heart turned over with grief. I knew I had to do something.

Why me? I wondered.

I stepped carefully around the rivulets of blood and walked over to the first small outline. It was a baby. I knelt down in the pool of blood and carefully lifted the outline. Somehow it weighed heavily in my hands.

How can that be?

I felt tears running down my cheeks and I wanted nothing more than to be able to hold this tiny form close against me and take its pain away. Was this a boy or a girl? I would never know, but somehow, it was important to me. I laid the form down gently in a crib and then picked up the others. The outlines of the babies were easy to pick up, but those of the toddlers were heavier and I was afraid I would drop them.

How dumb, I thought. *How can I drop something that isn't even here?*

When the outlines of all seven children were put into their beds, the most amazing thing happened. There was a swooshing sound and the blood began to recede until it was gone. The floor and walls were spotless, and the cribs and beds were white as snow bunnies. The outlines became figures of the babies and toddlers, and the pure white blankets humped up as though covering small bodies.

The blue mist figure glided toward me, and even though I know how stupid it sounds, I felt a kiss on my cheek. In the next moment, the mist swirled around in a fairy dance and disappeared. A second later, the flickering candles went out, one by one, until the room was dark.

Brianna, Talyn, Forest, and I stood and looked at each other.

Brianna said in a quavering voice, "Alexis, look! All the blood on you is gone, too!"

She was right. My hands and clothes were clean.

I said, "Come on, let's get out of here!"

We sprinted down the staircase - which had mysteriously reappeared - and scrambled over one another in our hurry to get out the front door. We threw the iron gate opened and then stopped in amazement. The moon had come out and it shone down on a clearly marked dirt road that led from the mansion, around the edge of the woods, to town. We hadn't had to come through the woods to find this place after all! We didn't stop to remark on this, however, we just raced down the road until our pounding hearts made us stop. Before our breathing was back to normal, we heard a howling that quickly became a shriek, like some gigantic animal in pain. Startled, we turned in the direction of the old house.

Dust rose up, turning into a faint blue mist as we watched, and then disappeared into the night.

The mansion, with all its monstrous secrets, was gone.

WHAT DWELLS BENEATH
ANTHONY GIANGREGORIO

"No way, I'm not going in there," Brett Masters said as he stared at the abandoned ice-skating rink.

"What's the matter? Scared?" Mark Addison asked with a devious grin.

"No, that's not it," Brett replied.

"Then what?"

Brett scrunched his forehead into multiple creases as he tried to come up with an excuse not to follow Mark into the dilapidated building. The truth was, he *was* scared to go in there. As he stared at the broken windows and cracked concrete he felt an unsettling feeling in his stomach, like a hundred butterflies had just woken up and were now all fluttering around within him.

Brett studied the two story structure, its peeling paint, its trash and debris strewn parking lot. Remnants from homeless people to teenagers who drank beer on the weekends, to regular citizens that had snuck in at night and dumped yard waste, couches, refrigerators and ovens. Even a few microwaves and television sets, their screens shattered, looking like eye sockets without the eyes, adorned the outside of the building.

There was so much trash the area around the ice skating rink resembled a junkyard. There were plans to tear it down and build apartments or condominiums, but something with the back taxes had put the development on hold. That's what Brett had heard his father and mother talking about one day when he had asked about the old rink. They had warned him never to go in there, not to even play around it.

The area was dangerous. Some of the flooring had become rotten from the leaky roof, and if he got hurt, there would be no one around to help him.

Of course, he hadn't heeded their advice and had hung out around the outside with Mark. The two boys searching through the trash to find some true treasures.

They had found a large piece of plywood and on one side someone had painted a large black and white skull. Mark had taken it home and had cut the skull out of the wood. After the two boys had built a go cart out of shopping carriage wheels and scrap wood, Mark had nailed the skull to the back of the go cart.

They had taken turns pushing each other around, a simple string used to steer the cart. Pull to the right and the wheel would be turned, the one bolt in the center of the two-by-four allowing for easy control.

But eventually they grew bored and had returned to the skating rink. This time Mark wanted to go inside.

They had never gone inside before, and though they knew deep down it was dangerous, the draw of mystery and adventure only a few blocks from home seemed exciting and safe at the same time.

"Then, what is it? *If* you're not scared?" Mark asked again, breaking Brett from his reverie.

Brett weighed his options and realized he had no choice. If he chickened out and didn't go inside with Mark, he knew his friend would never let him live it down. Every time the two would be at odds, Brett knew Mark would use the time he didn't go into the rink against him.

Though Brett knew with all his heart it was a mistake to go inside, he still turned to Mark, crossed his arms and said, "Never mind. I'll go with you."

Mark's face lit up with excitement and he slapped Brett on the shoulder. "All right, that's awesome. Come on, let's go. I can't wait to see what's in there."

Brett watched his friend walk away, and when Mark stopped, seeing Brett wasn't moving, his eyes went up and his hands went out before him as if to say, *well, come on then.*

Brett began walking as Mark turned and continued onward. Brett looked up at the daunting building as he moved closer, seeing the cracked shell and wrecked walls as something more than just a structure. The closer he got to it, now that he knew he was going inside, the more it seemed like a giant monster waiting to devour him.

He felt a tingle go down his spine and he hoped it was just nerves and not some kind of omen of what was to come.

As the two boys entered the skating rink from the west side, both of them let their mouths go slack as they stared at the inside of the decrepit structure.

The building was more than thirty years old, six of those years being abandoned, and there was refuse everywhere.

There was a second floor on one side of the building and the boys went to the stairs, slowly walking up the creaking steps. When they entered the first hallway, they found office space, still with cabinets and desks. Old files and manila envelops were scattered across the floor in each office, as if someone had been searching for something. With the windows broken, water had seeped in each time it rained and many places near the windows were water damaged; the floor uneven and in a few places the planks had begun to rise and crack.

Remains of animals were here and there, small bird skeletons as well as rat droppings. The air had an *off* smell to it, as if something old had combined with something dead, and that had joined with something wet. The aroma caused each boy to cover their noses and not talk.

Moving from office to office, kicking items out of the way with the tips of their sneakers, they soon began to grow bored.

Mark, the leader of the expedition, led Brett back down to the main floor, where the rink was.

Trash was piled in every curved corner. Dented, rusted shopping carts and blown leaves the predominant items. Beer bottles were second, as well as small liquor bottles. Many were broken and shattered, the small glass shards twinkled in the faint light, as if giving homage to the ice that once covered the forgotten surface.

The two boys walked around the rink, kicking anything that seemed interesting.

Brett was growing increasingly unsettled and was about to tell Mark he'd had enough and was going to leave, when Mark led them to the far end of the skating rink.

There was a small staircase there, made of poured cement, no more than four stairs high. As Mark looked down the stairs, he saw it led into a dark service tunnel that seemed to lead under the building.

"Cool, I wonder where this goes," Mark said as he and Brett peered into the Stygian darkness. Other than the few feet of light that penetrated the opening, the tunnel was an absolute mystery.

"No idea. Look, Mark, I think we've seen enough. I want to leave," Brett said hesitantly.

"What? Why? Not now. I just found this cool tunnel! This is so awesome! It must go all the way into the ground. Imagine what's under there."

Brett didn't want to think what was in the dark tunnel. Though he knew monsters weren't real, staring into the inky blackness, he had to admit, if they were real, then that's where one or more would want to live.

"Just think about it, Brett," Mark began. "No one's probably been in this tunnel for years. We can be like those explorers in Africa, who knows what we might find in there!"

"Yeah, that's what I'm afraid of," Brett said under his breath.

"What was that?"

"Nothing, I didn't say anything," Brett said. "Look, Mark, even if we wanted to go in there, we don't have a flashlight or anything."

"I have my lighter."

"A lighter won't do it and you know it. It'll get too hot after a few minutes and then where will we be?" Brett reasoned.

Mark gave that some thought and he let his eyes play over the floor. After a few seconds of looking, he went and picked up a two foot pipe, one of a half dozen littering the ground. He kicked a few items with the tip of his left sneaker before picking up a shirt. It had been blue once, but now it was faded to the point the color was almost gone. Bits of leaves, dried bugs, and dirt clung to all parts of it. Mark wrapped it around the top of the pipe, and when he was finished, he used his lighter and lit a stray piece of fabric jutting out to the side. It took a few seconds before the shirt began to burn, and as the makeshift torch flared to life, Mark beamed at Brett proudly. "There, now we can see. Come on, let's go check it out and when we're through, we can leave."

Though Brett knew he should say no, the truth was, as he looked at Mark standing there with a torch, the flames crackling, his friend looked like an adventurer from a movie. Brett couldn't help but feel some of that excitement as well, and being a normal boy, the call of mystery was too much to ignore. Against his better judgment Brett nodded and walked over to Mark. Both boys stood at the top of the small stairwell, looking down into the dark depths they prepared to take the plunge.

"Okay, let's go in a bit. But when I say I want to leave, we leave," Brett said.

"Fair enough. We'll go as far as we think it's safe, then we'll come back," Mark agreed.

Holding the torch before him, Mark began to descend the stairs, Brett right behind him.

* * *

The acrid stench of the burning shirt caused Brett to cover his nose with his shirtsleeve.

They had gone far enough into the service tunnel that the light at the opening was gone. This was due to the fact that the tunnel had been slowly curving downward for more than five minutes.

The floor was covered in more trash. Soda and beer cans, newspapers from ten years ago, and more rat droppings. Each step the two boys took sent debris rattling out of the way.

"Okay, Mark, we've gone far enough. I want to go back now," Brett said nervously.

"No way, this is so cool. I wonder how deep it goes." Mark asked as he stepped over a pile of refuse.

"I don't want to know. I want to leave," Brett said. "Come on, Mark, you said we'd go in and when I wanted to leave, we would."

Mark stopped walking, the torch illuminating his face in flickering shadows. The oily smoke roiled over their heads and floated down the tunnel, following the slight breeze. "I know what I said, but I changed my mind. I want to keep going." He smiled then, an evil smile, a knowing smile. "You can go if you want. I won't stop you."

"But I don't have a light. I won't be able to see."

"Exactly," Mark said.

"Fine, then give me your lighter," Brett demanded.

Mark shook his head. "No way. That's mine and I'm not giving it up."

"You're being a jerk you know."

Mark shrugged. "Maybe. So, what's it gonna be? You staying or going?"

"Like you don't know," Brett said angrily.

Mark turned and began walking and Brett stared at the back of his friend's head, his jaw tight with anger. Mark was being such a jerk. He began walking, following Mark again.

The two boys continued for another five minutes and the torch began to grow dim, flickering badly as it prepared to go out.

"Uh-oh, need some more fuel," Mark said. He lowered the torch to the floor and began searching for something to burn. It only took a few seconds before he found a dirty red and yellow scarf. Picking it up, he slowly wrapped it around the torch. At first it looked like the flame might go out, snuffed by the new material, but a second later it was burning brighter than before.

"There we go. Good as new," Mark said with a smile.

Brett said nothing, feeling like a prisoner, trapped deep inside the tunnel. With no light, there was no way he was going to try and leave the tunnel alone. It was a long walk back and though he could hold onto the wall, the imagery of being in complete darkness was too much to consider.

As they walked, the trash began to thin. Conduits that ran along the wall near the ceiling began to dwindle until they were gone completely.

"Gees, how far down does this thing go?" Mark asked, his voice echoing off the walls.

Brett looked at the ceiling, and another shiver filled him. He felt as if he was a thousand miles underground, the weight of the world over his head. He had a vision of an earthquake, of the ceiling cracking and tons of concrete and dirt falling in on him, crushing him, burying him. He realized his mom and dad would never know where he was. He would be buried alive, then he would die and no one would know he was down here. Served him right, he thought. He never should have come down here. What was he thinking?

Suddenly he wanted his mom more than anything, to feel her arms around him, her soft voice telling him it would be all right. But she wasn't here. He was alone with Mark. He had to be strong. He had to stay calm and sooner or later Mark would get bored and they would leave. He knew once he was free of the tunnel he would never come within ten feet of the skating rink again.

He had learned his lesson well.

Mark stopped walking and kicked something with his sneaker.

"Hey, look at this," he said to Brett as he knelt down to inspect the item.

Brett looked despite himself. The sooner he pleased Mark, the sooner he would want to leave. Brett looked at what Mark had found and he blinked into the flickering light, not believing what he saw.

"No way," Brett whispered. "It can't be."

Mark reached down with his free hand and picked up the item he'd found. "Sure looks like it to me. I had to get a physical last month and there was a skeleton in the doctor's office. I was bored so I was messing with it. This looks like the arm of that skeleton."

Brett made a raspberry. "That's crazy. It must be a mistake."

"I don't know, looks pretty real to me."

Brett began to get scared. "Gees, Mark, if it's true then we need to get out of here right now. We need to tell someone, the police, my parents."

"Whoa there, Sport. Look at this thing. It's old, real old. Probably been down here for years. There's no rush. I say we leave it here and we can take it back with us when we leave."

"Why don't we leave now?" Brett asked.

"Because this is getting good, that's why." Mark began walking further down the tunnel, dropping the ulna bone on the ground.

Brett looked at it for a second before he hurried to keep up with Mark. Like it or not, Mark was his lifeline.

* * *

They found more human bones as they went deeper into the tunnel, and the floor began to grow steeper, continuing into the earth. Some of the bones they now found didn't look so old. More than one looked like they had teeth marks on them, like they had been chewed by an animal that was trying to get the marrow within.

And then the cement walls were gone, to be replaced by hard-packed dirt.

"Okay, Mark, this is as far as I go. There's no more tunnel left."

"What are you talking about? There's still a tunnel and I want to see where it goes. This is so awesome! We're probably the first people down here in like ten years!"

"But, Mark, what about the bones? They had to get here somehow. Please, for me, can we go back now?" Brett pleaded.

Mark shook his head. "No way. I want to see what's at the end of this tunnel. Maybe it's some secret society, like cannibals or something. Maybe there's like people from a hundred years ago. You know, like mole people. They have white eyes and they can't see 'cause they live in the dark. Wow, can you imagine that? We'd be heroes, finding this new species of people right in our own backyard."

"But, Mark. . ." Brett protested.

"But nothing," Mark said, his voice firm. "We keep going. When we get to the end, we'll go back, not before." He pushed past Brett and made his way down the tunnel.

Brett bit his lip, wishing he had the courage to just leave, to go back even though it was pitch black. But he couldn't, not yet anyway.

Turning, Brett followed the flickering torch ahead of him.

* * *

More minutes past and the air grew cool and the sound of dripping water came to their ears.

The tunnel was still going downward, and as it curved to the left, the two boys found it had come to a junction.

Before them was a wide open space, about the size of an average living room. Like the tunnel, it was carved from the earth, the sides made of hard-packed dirt and clay. To support the ceiling, odd sized, leftover pieces of wood were propped as rafters. In the far corner, lost in the shadows, the dripping was slightly louder.

"Whoa, will you look at this?" Mark said, his eyes wide with amazement. He moved the torch back and forth, illuminating the cave. When he reached the far right, he stopped moving, his mouth falling open in awe. Brett saw what the torch's feeble light had brought into view and he was speechless, the terror itching at his back again, making his legs shake.

On the floor of the cave, scattered about like trash, were piles of human bones. Many were cracked in half, as if a giant animal had fed on the marrow within. All had scrapes and gouges on their smooth surfaces, and not one had so much as a scrap of flesh remaining. In the pile, a few grinning, bleached skulls glared back at the two boys, as if accusing them of invading their inner sanctum.

Something lived here, something that ate people!

"Oh my God, Mark, those are bones! We need to leave, right now."

"Why? There's no one here. This place looks abandoned. For all we know these old bones have been here for decades. We're fine," Mark said, though his eyes were moving around faster as he peered into the shadows just out of reach of the torch's perimeter.

"I don't care. I want to go. . . right now." Brett was adamant and was considering just turning and running, not caring about the darkness any more, his desperation to escape stronger than his fear.

Mark ignored Brett's pleadings. He felt immune to the threat of potential danger. After all, he was a kid. What could happen to him?

Brett was about to reply, to try and plead his case yet again for leaving, when a scuffing sound came from somewhere in the cave.

"What was that?" Brett asked, his voice shaking.

Mark didn't reply. He stood stock still. Brett was about to speak again when the scuffing echoed to them once more. Mark raised the torch higher and took a few steps into the center of the cave. As the light pushed back the darkness it exposed another tunnel on the far side of the cave. It was smaller than the one they had used to enter and it went even deeper into the earth. As the two boys stared in silence, fear eating at their insides, a scraping sound could be hard. . . and it was coming from the other tunnel.

Swallowing the knot in his throat, Mark turned to look at Brett. "I think we can leave now," he said nervously.

Brett only nodded and began backing away from the other tunnel, Mark right behind him. Meanwhile, the scraping, scuffing grew in pitch, and as the two boys were about to turn and run, a misshapen form appeared at the opening to the tunnel at the opposite end of the cave. Mark and Brett could only see the creature in dull outlines. Brett blinked repeatedly as he stared, not believing what he saw. The creature was hunched over, like it had a bad back, and it was bald with the exception of a few scraggly wisps of white hair. It was human, or humanoid, though its arms and legs seemed shorter, squatter than a standard human being. Its exposed flesh was devoid of hair, only a pair of shorts, covered in dirt and grime, adorning its pale body.

Pale was an understatement. The skin was so white it seemed to glow in the dark, the skin color the same as the eyes. Both orbs were bone white, and if it could see, Brett wondered how. As the two boys took a step backwards, the head of the creature turned sharply, telling Brett it may not be able to see at all, but hunted by sound alone, which made sense in the darkness of the tunnels.

As it homed in on the two boys like a bat, it opened its mouth wide to expose pointed yellow and brown teeth, the incisors flashing in the dim light of the torch.

Without warning the creature lunged for them.

"Go, go, it's coming!" Mark yelled as Brett turned and began to run into the tunnel they had used to enter the cave, his hands out before him as he plunged into the darkness. Behind him, Mark followed, the torch jumping up and down in his hand, causing the light to barely penetrate in front of Brett.

But there was no time for Brett to stop and let Mark get ahead of him nor did Brett want to do so. As he ran, he could hear Mark's footsteps behind him and beyond that, the hissing and scraping as the creature followed them.

Everything became a blur for Brett as he stumbled up the tunnel. As he now ascended, his legs began to hurt, but he ignored the pain, only wanting to be free of the tunnel and its cannibalistic dweller.

"Hurry up, Brett! It's right behind me!" Mark yelled as he pushed at Brett, who stumbled forward.

Righting himself, Brett tried to run faster, his hands sliding along the dirt walls as he tried not to hyperventilate. He was so scared. He had never, ever been this scared in his life. His heart was beating so fast it was like a jungle drum in his head and his stomach was filled with more than a million butterflies. He felt like he had to go to the bathroom but he ignored it, only wanting to break free of the tomb he now found himself in.

Behind him, Brett could hear Mark's heavy breathing and every now and then low sobs. Mark was crying, his facade of bravery now gone. Brett didn't hold it against him, in fact he wanted to cry too.

The two boys were more than halfway through the tunnel, and had just past the area where the walls had been made of dirt and had once more become concrete, when Mark let out a piercing yell and fell heavily to the tunnel floor. The torch fell from his hand and rolled a few feet to lie in the dirt. Luckily, it didn't go out, though its brightness went down by more than half. In the half light the tunnel was nothing but gloom and shadows.

Brett turned around to try and help his friend, but when he spun about, he was able to look deeper into the tunnel and over Mark's prone body. His breath lodged in his chest at what he saw.

The creature was there, the ghoul, as Brett called it in his mind, for what else could it be but a ghoul? It lived underground and ate humans. And as no one had been reported missing, the remains had to be of dead people. There was a cemetery not more than a mile away and Brett wondered if the other tunnel went all the way to the graveyard. After traversing what seemed like hundreds of feet of tunnel the idea didn't seem so farfetched.

The ghoul stopped right behind Mark, seeming to stare at Brett in accusation. It cocked its head to the side, its mouth opening slightly and Brett could imagine what it wanted to say. *"How dare you come into my home uninvited?"*

Mark was crying now, and as he tried to get up, he fell back down. His ankle was sprained; he was wounded, like an old zebra at the end of the herd, the lion waiting for it to straggle to the end of the line so it could pounce.

Mark's face was a rictus of pain and he didn't realize the ghoul was behind him. With tears rolling down his cheeks Mark reached up with his left hand, "Help me up, Brett. My ankle. . . I can't walk."

Brett couldn't move as he stared at the ghoul behind Mark, and slowly Mark realized Brett wasn't looking at him. Finally, Mark rolled onto his side and looked behind him. He peered up at the ghoul and let out a loud scream that bounced off the walls of the tunnel.

As Brett watched in horror the ghoul bent over and grabbed Mark by his ankles, causing Mark to scream yet again. It began dragging Mark deeper into the tunnel, back to its lair of bones and dirt.

"No, don't let it take me! Help me Brett! I don't want to go! I want my mommy! Help meeee!"

With arms and hands outstretched like a drowning man, Mark was dragged into the darkness until he vanished from sight, the light of the torch only penetrating a few feet in either direction. Brett was still too scared to move and he knew if the ghoul wanted him as well, it could easily take him. The sounds of Mark's body being dragged on the tunnel floor continued, as did his screams.

His pleadings for help and mercy never stopped. His sobs for his mom and dad never ceasing until finally a chilling sound came to Brett's ears that he would never forget, no matter how long he lived.

Mark was in mid-yell, his wails so loud they filled the tunnel like a living thing and then, as if a light switch had been flicked, they ceased. But that wasn't the sound that haunted Brett. Just before the cries of his friend stopped, there was a dull cracking sound, similar to the sound a finger thick tree branch would make when it was broken over a knee. Like the breaking of a neck.

Then there was silence, followed by the sound of more dragging which soon faded away. Soon, Brett could only hear his breathing and his heartbeat pounding as adrenalin filled him to the point he was going to explode, but still he couldn't move.

Finally, shaking himself free of terror, he reached down, picked up the torch, and began running as fast as he could. At a half-jog, half-run he proceeded through the tunnel, towards the surface.

It seemed to take forever, but eventually he reached the exit. As he came out of the tunnel and into the skating rink, he dropped the torch into the accumulated dirt where it was extinguished, and ran all the way home.

When he was asked by his mother why he looked so scared, he said he was almost hit by a car. It was accepted as true and he went to his room, where he hid in his closet for the rest of the night, too scared to come out.

The next day the word went out at school that Mark was missing. No one knew what had happened to him and foul play was suspected, perhaps a kidnapping though the boy running away from home wasn't ruled out. Apparently Mark had an argument with his father the night before.

Brett never told another soul what had happened under the skating rink, for who would believe him? He knew anyone he told would merely say it was the rantings of an overactive imagination.

Six months later, the ice skating rink was torn down and condominiums were built. If any of the demolition crew found an underground cave, human bones, or Mark, Brett never heard about it.

As the years went by, Brett even made himself believe it was all a dream, that it had never happened. But late at night, when the moon was full and the darkness enveloped the land, he would look out his window and sometimes, if he looked just right, he believed he saw a humanoid shape in the shadows at the edge of his yard, watching him, waiting.

Waiting for the one that got away.

ABOUT THE WRITERS

Rebecca Besser lives in Ohio with her husband and little man. She's a graduate of the Institute of Children's Literature, a member of Write-On Writers and the Ohio Poetry Association. Her writing has appeared in the Coshocton Tribune, Irish Story Playhouse, Spaceports & Spidersilk, joyful!, Soft Whispers, Illuminata, Common Threads, Golden Visions Magazine, and she has multiple stories in anthologies by Living Dead Press, where she is now an editor. Her website: www.rebeccabesser.com

Anthony Giangregorio is the author and editor of more than 45 novels, almost all of them about zombies. His work has appeared in Dead Science by Coscomentertainment, Dead Worlds: Undead Stories Volumes 1-6, and Wolves of War by Library of the Living Dead Press. He also has stories in End of Days Vol. 1-3, the Book of the Dead series Vol. 1-4 by LDP, and two anthologies with Pill Hill Press. He is also the creator of the popular action/zombie series titled "Deadwater." Check out his website at www.undeadpress.com.

Courtney Rene lives in the State of Ohio with her husband and two children. She has been an avid reader and writer since she was a small child, and in fact wrote her first story while in the second grade. You can still usually find her when she is not writing, with her nose in a book. Her favorite genres to read are fantasy and historical fiction. Please feel free to contact her at ctnyrene@aol.com

Mikki Sadil lives in a small Victorian town on the Central Coast of California with her husband, Welsh Corgi, Siamese/Himalayan cat, an African Gray parrot and a Blue-and-Gold Macaw. She is a retired professor of Sociological Statistics and Research Methodology, and retired horse trainer. She has been writing her whole life but specifically for children only in the last four years. She had a book of Haiku poetry published in college, and has had stories and articles published in national children's magazines since 2008. Mikki has completed two novels for Middle Grade/Young Adults, has a mystery novel about half finished, and is currently working on an historical fiction novel about the Civil War and the Underground Railroad.

Charles Versfelt is currently working on a thriller novel, the Jefferson Bible Code. He lives in New Jersey with his wife Doreen, daughter Kayla and stepdaughter Melissa.

PLAYING GOD: A ZOMBIE NOVEL
by Jeffery Dye

It was supposed to be a regeneration virus to help soldiers on the battle-field—regrowing limbs and healing wounds— but a simple act of carelessness unleashed it on an unsuspecting world.

For the virus was not perfected, and once exposed, the host quickly dies, only to rise again as one of the undead.

As countries are quickly overrun, scientists and military teams battle to contain the outbreak.

There is no other option.

If the infection continues to spread, soon the entire globe will be consumed. And perhaps that will be a just punishment for a mankind that dared to try to play God.

DEAD HOUSE: A ZOMBIE GHOST STORY
by Keith Adam Luethke

The old mansion on the edge of town, aptly named Dead House, has a history of blood, pain, and death, but what Victor Leeds knows of this past only scratches the surface of the true horrors within.

But when his girlfriend is attacked by a shadowy figure one rainy night, he soon finds himself caught up in a world where the dead walk and ghostly wraiths abound. And to make matters worse, a pair of serial killers are fulfilling carefully made plans, and when they are done, the small town of Stormville, New York will run red. The last ingredient to open the gates of Hell, and plunge this small upstate town into madness, is rain.   And in Stormville, it pours by the gallons.

The Lazarus Culture
by Pasquale J. Morrone

Secret Service Agent Christopher Kearns had no idea what he was up against. Assigned on a temporary basis to the Center for Disease Control, he only knew that somehow it was connected to the lives of those the agency protected...namely, the President of the United States. If there were possible terrorist activities in the making, he could only guess it was at a red alert basis.

When Kearns meets and befriends Doctor Marlene Peterson of the Breezy Point Medical Center in Maryland, he soon finds that science fiction can indeed become a reality. In a solitary room walked a man with no vital signs: dead. The explanation he received came from Doctor Lee Fret, a man assigned to the case from the CDC. Something was attached to the brain stem. Something alive that was quickly spreading rapidly through Maryland and other states.

Kearns and his ragtag army of agents and medical personnel soon find themselves in a world of meaningless slaughter and mayhem. The armies of the walking dead were far more than mere zombies. Some began to change into whatever it was they ate. The government had found a way to reanimate the dead by implanting a parasite found on the tongue of the Red Snapper to the human brain. It looked good on paper, but it was a project straight from Hell.

The dead now walked, but it wasn't a mystery. It was The Lazarus Culture.

DEAD RAGE

by Anthony Giangregorio
Book 2 in the Rage virus series!

An unknown virus spreads across the globe, turning ordinary people into bloodthirsty, ravenous killers.

Only a small percentage of the population is immune and soon become prey to the infected.

Amongst the infected comes a man, stricken by the virus, yet still retaining his grasp on reality. His need to destroy the *normals* becomes an obsession and he raises an army of killers to seek out and kill all who aren't *changed* like himself. A few survivors gather together on the outskirts of Chicago and find themselves running for their lives as the specter of death looms over all.

The Dead Rage virus will find you, no matter where you hide.

CHRISTMAS IS DEAD: A ZOMBIE ANTHOLOGY

Edited by Anthony Giangregorio

Twas the night before Christmas and all through the house, not a creature was stirring, not even a. . . zombie?

That's right; this anthology explores what would happen at Christmas time if there was a full blown zombie outbreak. Reanimated turkeys, zombie Santas, and demon reindeers that turn people into flesh-eating ghouls are just some of the tales you will find in this merry undead book. So curl up under the Christmas tree with a cup of hot chocolate, and as the fireplace crackles with warmth, get ready to have your heart filled with holiday cheer. But of course, then it will be ripped from your heaving chest and fed upon by blood-thirsty elves with a craving for human flesh! For you see, Christmas is Dead!

And you will never look at the holiday season the same way again.

BLOOD RAGE
(The Prequel to DEAD RAGE)

by Anthony Giangregorio

The madness descended before anyone knew what was happening. Perfectly normal people suddenly became rage-fueled killers, tearing and slicing their way across the city. Within hours, Chicago was a battlefield, the dead strewn in the streets like trash.

Stacy, Chad and a few others are just a few of the immune, unaffected by the virus but not to the violence surrounding them. The *changed* are ravenous, sweeping across Chicago and perhaps the world, destroying any *normals* they come across. Fire, slaughter, and blood rule the land, and the few survivors are now an endangered species.

This is the story of the first days of the Dead Rage virus and the brave souls who struggle to live just one more day.

When the smoke clears, and the *changed* have maimed and killed all who stand in their way, only the strong will remain.   The rest will be left to rot in the sun.

DEAD END: A ZOMBIE NOVEL
by Anthony Giangregorio
THE DEAD WALK!

Newspapers everywhere proclaim the dead have returned to feast on the living!

A small group of survivors hole up in a cellar, afraid to brave the masses of animated corpses, but when food runs out, they have no choice but to venture out into a world gone mad.

What they will discover, however, is that the fall of civilization has brought out the worst in their fellow man.

Cannibals, psychotic preachers and rapists are just some of the atrocities they must face.

In a world turned upside down, it is life that has hit a Dead End.

DEADFREEZE
by Anthony Giangregorio
THIS IS WHAT HELL WOULD BE LIKE IF IT FROZE OVER!

When an experimental serum for hypothermia goes horribly wrong, a small research station in the middle of Antarctica becomes overrun with an army of the frozen dead.

Now a small group of survivors must battle the arctic weather and a horde of frozen zombies as they make their way across the frozen plains of Antarctica to a neighboring research station.

What they don't realize is that they are being hunted by an entity whose sole reason for existing is vengeance; and it will find them wherever they run.

VISIONS OF THE DEAD
A ZOMBIE STORY
by Anthony & Joseph Giangregorio

Jake Roberts felt like he was the luckiest man alive.

He had a great family, a beautiful girlfriend, who was soon to be his wife, and a job, that might not have been the best, but it paid the bills.

At least until the dead began to walk.

Now Jake is fighting to survive in a dead world while searching for his lost love, Melissa, knowing she's out there somewhere.

But the past isn't dead, and as he struggles for an uncertain future, the past threatens to consume him. With the present a constant battle between the living and the dead, Jake finds himself slipping in and out of the past, the visions of how it all happened haunting him. But Jake knows Melissa is out there somewhere and he'll find her or die trying.

In a world of the living dead, you can never escape your past.

INSIDE THE PERIMETER: SCAVENGERS OF THE DEAD

by Alan Spencer

In the middle of nowhere, the vestiges of an abandoned town are surrounded by inescapably high concrete barriers, permitting no trespass or escape. The town is dormant of human life, but rampant with the living dead, who choose not to eat flesh, but to instead continue their survival by cruder means.

Boyd Broman, a detective arrested and falsely imprisoned, has been transferred into the secret town. He is given an ultimatum: recapture Hayden Grubaugh, the cannibal serial killer, who has been banished to the town, in exchange for his freedom.

During Boyd's search, he discovers why the psychotic cannibal must really be captured and the sinister secrets the dead town holds.

With no chance of escape, Broman finds himself trapped among the ravenous, violent dead.

With the cannibal feeding on the animated cadavers and the undead searching for Boyd, he must fulfill his end of the deal before the rotting corpses turn him into an unwilling organ donor.

But Boyd wasn't told that no one gets out alive, that the town is a death sentence.

For there is no escape from *Inside the Perimeter*.

DEADFALL

by Anthony Giangregorio

It's Halloween in the small suburban town of Wakefield, Mass.

While parents take their children trick or treating and others throw costume parties, a swarm of meteorites enter the earth's atmosphere and crash to earth.

Inside are small parasitic worms, no larger than maggots.

The worms quickly infect the corpses at a local cemetery and so begins the rise of the undead.

The walking dead soon get the upper hand, with no one believing the truth. That the dead now walk.

Will a small group of survivors live through the zombie apocalypse?

Or will they, too, succumb to the Deadfall.

LOVE IS DEAD: A ZOMBIE ANTHOLOGY

Edited by Anthony Giangregorio

THE DEATH OF LOVE

Valentine's Day is a day when young love is fulfilled.

Where hopeful young men bring candy and flowers to their sweethearts, in hopes of a kiss...or perhaps more. But not in this anthology.

For you see, LOVE IS DEAD, and in this tome, the dead walk, wanting to feed on those same hearts that once pumped in chests, bursting with love.

So toss aside that heart-shaped box of candy and throw away those red roses, you won't need them any longer. Instead, strap on a handgun, or pick up a shotgun and defend yourself from the ravenous undead.

Because in a world where the dead walk, even love isn't safe.

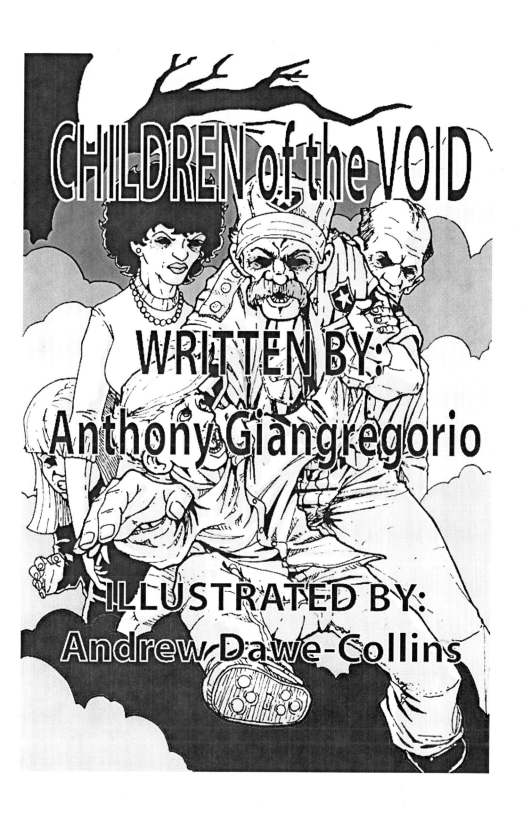

CPSIA information can be obtained at www.ICGtesting.com
Printed in the USA
BVOW04s1725070514

352784BV00008B/93/P